The Lucky Leopard

Adapted from an original southern African folklore tale

Retold by Andrea Florens

Illustrated by Claire Norden

Long, long ago in Africa,
there lived a leopard.
His name was Lengau
and he was the biggest,
most beautiful leopard in the land.

Not far from the Leopard's home, there lived an old king.
The king was very **troubled** because he could not sleep.
He was so tired, but still the poor old king could not fall asleep.
He called all the wise men in his kingdom to find the answer
that would help him to fall asleep. Only
one **wise** man had an answer.

This wise man told him to cover himself with the skin coat of an animal. But, it could not be just any animal, it had to be the skin of the biggest, most beautiful leopard in the land. With this skin covering him from head to toe, he would fall asleep immediately! And so the king sent his warriors to find the **biggest, most beautiful** leopard in the land.

After two long days of searching, the warriors found a
waterhole. And what did they see on the other side?
The biggest, most beautiful leopard
they had ever seen!

Quickly, one of the warriors grabbed his assegai and threw it
with all his might.
It landed with a great thud next to Lengau's paw.

The chase began...
Lengau leaping from tree to tree,
as fast as he could, but the warriors and their dogs
were always just behind him.

Eventually, Lengau managed to get away
from the warriors and their dogs.
The sun had gone and the night was dark.
Exhausted and scared, poor Lengau sat high up on a rock and
wondered what to do to save himself.

Just at that moment he heard
the wild **laughing of Hyena**
across the valley.

Now Lengau was not very fond of Hyena,
but he knew that Hyena was a clever
creature so he decided to ask him for help.

Hee Hee!
Hee!

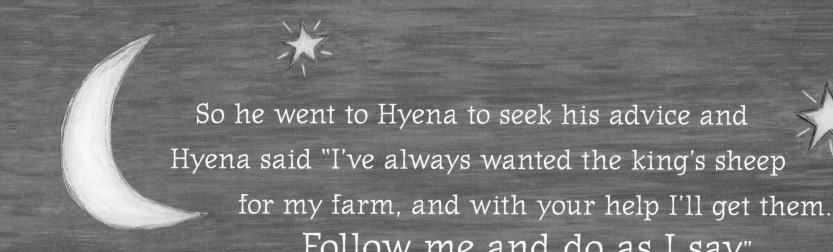

So he went to Hyena to seek his advice and
Hyena said "I've always wanted the king's sheep
for my farm, and with your help I'll get them.
Follow me and do as I say".
Off they went to the king's village where they stole five
of the king's woolliest sheep and lead them back
to Hyena's sheep farm.

Hyena then told Lengau to go and hide.

The next night, Hyena, came to Lengau's **hiding** place. And there Hyena unrolled the most beautiful leopard skin before his eyes. Lengau was **confused**, but Hyena laughed and told Lengau how his wives had cut the wool off the sheep and had sewn and painted it to **look like** a leopard's skin.

Hyena then called his friends the owls,
who picked up the fake leopard skin and flew
to the warriors, who were so exhausted from
the chase, that they were fast asleep.

The owls then carefully laid the skin next to the sleeping men and flew away.

The next morning the warriors couldn't believe their luck!
How the biggest, most beautiful leopard skin came to
them, they did not know, but their exhausting
search was over.

Back to the king's village they went, the biggest, most
beautiful leopard skin in their arms.
The king was overjoyed!

He praised the warriors and rewarded them with a feast.

Then the king hurried off to his bedroom and covered himself from head to toe in the **biggest, most beautiful** leopard skin he had ever seen.

Later that night, the king's snores could be heard for **miles** and **miles** around.

Lengau sat high on a rock that night.
When he heard the snores of the king, he took a deep
breath in and out, and he lay down to rest.

How **lucky** he was,
safe again in his
big and beautiful
spotted skin.

Published in South Africa by Art Pub Printing (Pty) Ltd t/a Art Publishers
Reg. No 2018/329395/07
61 Stewart Street, Townsend Estate
Goodwood, Cape Town, 7460
Tel: +27 21 532 3020
www.artpublishers.co.za

First Published 2009
Second Revised Edition 2015